THE
PRINCESS
AND THE
PIG

For Caroline, who knows the sort of things
that happen all the while in books —J. E.
For my friend María Oms and her love for books —P. B.

Originally published in Great Britain by Macmillan Children's Books in September 2011
First published in the United States of America in September 2011
by Walker Books for Young Readers, an imprint of Bloomsbury Publishing, Inc.
www.bloomsbury.com

Bloomsbury is a registered trademark of Bloomsbury Publishing Plc

For information about permission to reproduce selections from this book, write to
Permissions, Bloomsbury Children's Books, 1385 Broadway, New York, New York 10018
Bloomsbury books may be purchased for business or promotional use. For information on bulk purchases
please contact Macmillan Corporate and Premium Sales Department at specialmarkets@macmillan.com

Library of Congress Cataloging-in-Publication Data
Emmett, Jonathan.
The princess and the pig / by Jonathan Emmett ; illustrated by Poly Bernatene.—1st U.S. ed.
p. cm.
Summary: When a new baby princess accidentally changes places with a piglet,
both of their lives are forever changed.
ISBN 978-0-8027-2334-5 (hardcover) • ISBN 978-0-8027-2335-2 (reinforced)
[1. Princesses—Fiction. 2. Pigs—Fiction. 3. Humorous stories.] I. Bernatene, Poly, ill. II. Title.
PZ7.E696Pr 2011 [E]—dc22 2010049549

Art created digitally • Typeset in Paqui
Printed in China by WKT, Shenzhen, Guangdong
5 7 9 10 8 6 (hardcover)
3 5 7 9 10 8 6 4 2 (reinforced)

All papers used by Bloomsbury Publishing, Inc., are natural, recyclable products made
from wood grown in well-managed forests. The manufacturing processes
conform to the environmental regulations of the country of origin.

THE PRINCESS AND THE PIG

Jonathan Emmett ★ Poly Bernatene

BLOOMSBURY
NEW YORK LONDON NEW DELHI SYDNEY

Not that long ago, in a kingdom not far from here, a farmer was traveling home from the market with a cartload of straw.

The farmer was so poor that he didn't have a horse and had to pull his own cart.

In the back of the cart lay a tiny pink piglet.

Nobody wanted to buy the piglet at the market,
but the farmer had taken pity on it.

"I'll call you Pigmella," he decided,
as this seemed like a good name for a pig.

It was a hot day and the farmer stopped to
rest in the shade of a great castle.
Far, far above him, on a high balcony, a queen
was inspecting her new baby daughter.

The queen was so rich that she had seven
nannies and didn't have to look after her own child.

The queen picked the baby out of
her cradle and held her at arm's length.

"I'll call it Priscilla," she decided,
as this seemed like a good
name for a princess.

A moment later, a wet, squelching noise came from the baby's diaper, closely followed by an awful smell.

"Yuck!" shrieked the queen, dropping the baby and running off to find the royal nannies.

She left so quickly that she didn't notice she had dropped the baby . . .

. . . over the edge of the balcony!

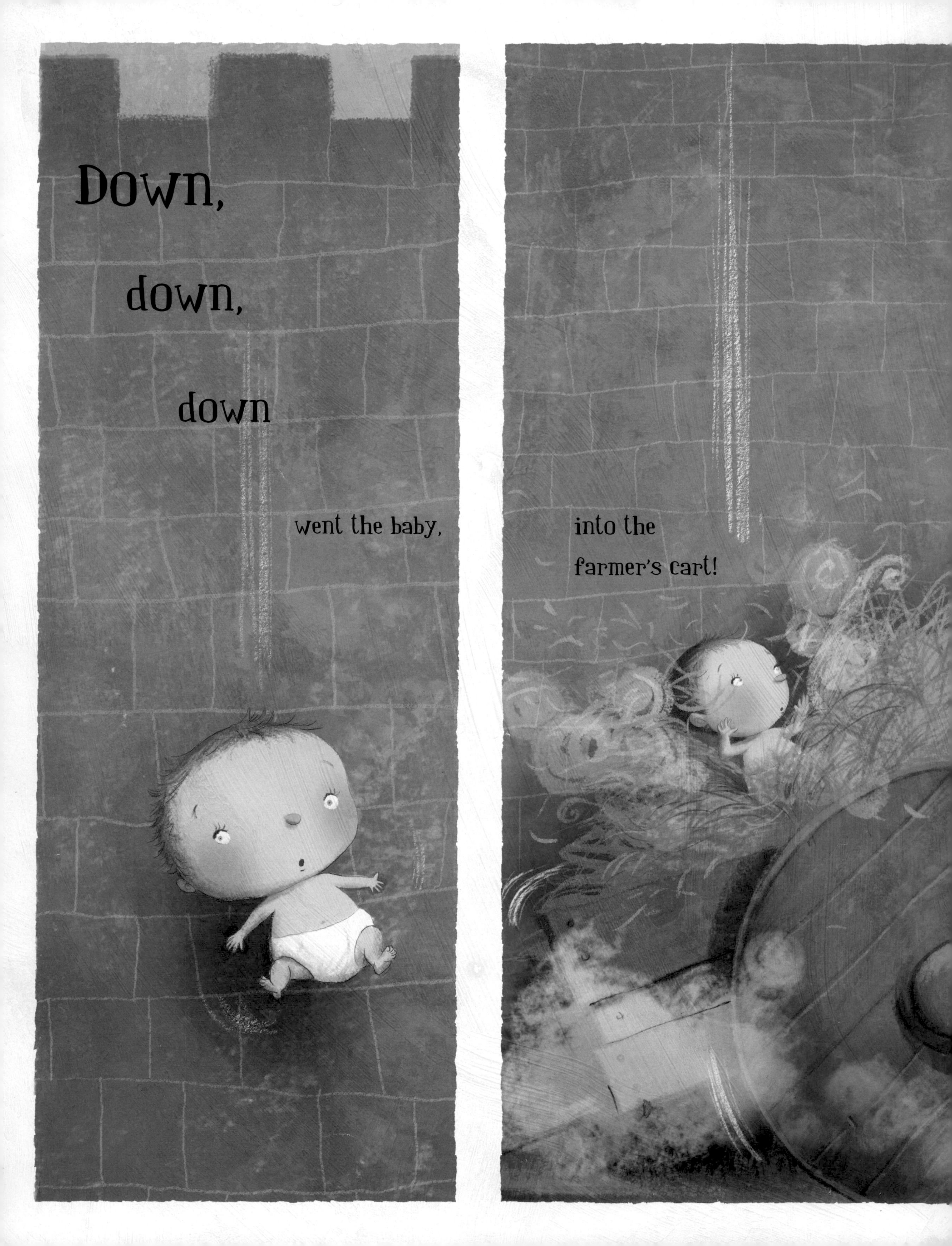

Down,

down,

down

went the baby,

into the

farmer's cart!

Up,

up,

up

flew the piglet,

into the princess's cradle!

When the queen returned and
found the piglet lying where
the baby should have been, she
let out an even louder shriek
and fainted into the nannies' arms.

The king thought he knew what had happened.

"A bad fairy has done this," he explained. "The fairy wasn't invited to the princess's christening, so she's turned the baby into a piglet to get her revenge. It's the sort of thing that happens all the time in books."

Meanwhile, the farmer had returned home and was surprised to discover a baby girl lying where the piglet should have been.

The farmer's wife thought she knew what had happened.

"A good fairy has done this," she explained. "The fairy knew how poor and honest we are and how badly we wanted a child, so she turned the piglet into a baby. It's the sort of thing that happens all the time in books."

And so, without a second thought, the baby
became Pigmella, the farmer's daughter.

And the piglet became Priscilla, the royal princess.

It wasn't long before Pigmella was able to . . .

And the farmer and his wife soon
forgot that she had ever been a pig.

Things were not so easy for Priscilla!

But the king and queen never let anyone
forget that she was really a princess.

As Pigmella grew older,

she grew smarter,

and beautiful,

and was **admired**
by everyone she met.

As Priscilla grew older,

she grew not so smart,

and not so beautiful,

and was **avoided** by
everyone she met.

Then, one day, the farmer's wife overheard some of the castle servants talking about the princess who had turned into a pig.

"It's just like what happened to Pigmella," she told her husband, "only the other way around."

The farmer soon guessed what had happened.

"The princess and the pig must have swapped places somehow," he explained. "It's the sort of thing that happens all the time in books."

The poor farmer and his wife were very unhappy. They loved Pigmella, but they knew they must return her to her rightful home.

Pigmella was also unhappy.
She loved the farmer and his wife and did not want to live with anyone else.

But they were an honest family, so the next day they all went to the castle to see the king and queen.

The king and queen
listened to the farmer's story . . .

But they didn't believe it!

"What nonsense!" cried the queen.

"Ridiculous!" The king laughed.

"This girl may be smart and beautiful, but she does not look or speak like a real princess."

The queen thought she knew what was happening.

"It's a trick," she declared. "This girl is just a farmer's daughter pretending to be a princess so that she can marry a prince. It's the sort of thing that happens all the time in books."

And so Pigmella returned home with the farmer and his wife, where she married a young shepherd and lived happily ever after—and never once wished that she'd been a princess.

And Priscilla also got married—to a handsome prince!
Although he had to be talked into it.

"Priscilla was changed into a pig by a bad fairy,"
the king explained.

"But once you kiss her, the spell will be broken and she
will turn back into a beautiful princess," added the queen.

"It's the sort of thing that happens all the time
in books," they assured him.

But, unfortunately for the prince . . .

. . . it's **not** the sort of thing that happens in this particular book.